W9-AUJ-045

© 2005 Bookmart Limited

All rights reserved. No part of this
publication may be reproduced,
stored in a retrieval system or
transmitted by any means,
electronic, mechanical,
photocopying or otherwise, without
the prior permission of the publisher.

Published by
Armadillo Books
an imprint of
Bookmart Limited
Registered Number 2372865
Trading as Bookmart Limited
Blaby Road
Wigston
Leicester LE18 4SE

ISBN 1-84322-410-0

Produced for
Bookmart Limited by
Nicola Baxter
PO Box 215
Framingham Earl
Norwich NR14 7UR

Designer: Amanda Hawkes
Production designer: Amy Barton
Illustrator: Daniel Howarth/Advocate

1 3 5 7 9 10 8 6 4 2

Printed in China

It's fun to read with the teddy bears!

Your child will already be familiar with the idea of teddy bears having a picnic! In this story, simple, repeated language and cheeky characters are ideal for encouraging your child's first steps in reading. The book can be used in several ways to help beginning readers gain confidence.

You could start by reading the illustrated words at the edge of each lefthand page with your child. Have fun trying to spot the same words in the story itself.

All the words on the righthand page have already been met on the facing page. Help your child to read these by pointing out words and groups of words already met.

Finally, all the illustrated words can be found at the end of the book. Enjoy checking all the words you can both read!

The Teddy Bears' Picnic

Written by Nicola Baxter · Illustrated by Daniel Howarth

ARMADILLO

bed

sun

sky

basket

One morning, Teddy Tim woke up in his little bed.

The sun was shining.

The sky was blue.

"This is a good day for a picnic!" said Teddy Tim.

He went to find a basket.

"This is a good basket for a picnic!"
said Teddy Tim.

cupboard

bananas

fridge

juice

"I must find something to eat at the picnic," said Teddy Tim.

He looked in a cupboard. "Oh no!" said Teddy Tim. "I can only see bananas."

He put them in his basket.

Teddy Tim looked in the fridge. "Oh no!" he said. "I can only see juice."

Teddy Tim put the juice
in his basket.

road

shop

plums

cherries

So Teddy Tim took his basket and set off down the road.

He saw his friend Teddy Tessa coming out of a shop.

"Hello, Teddy Tim! Where are you going?" she said.

"I'm going for a picnic," said Teddy Tim.

"Can I come?" said Tessa. "Look! I have some plums and some cherries."

"Yes, you can!" said Teddy Tim.

So Teddy Tim and Teddy Tessa
set off down the road.

garden

"Hello, Teddy Tim!
Hello, Teddy Tessa!"
said Teddy Eddy.
He was in the garden
in front of his house.

house

"Can you come for a picnic?"
said Teddy Tim.

"Yes! I can bring a melon
from my garden!" said Eddy.
"What have **you** got?"

melon

Tim looked into his basket.
"Fruit," he said.

"Lots of fruit,"
said Tessa.

gate

Teddy Eddy
opened his gate.
"I can help,"
he said.

Teddy Tim, Teddy Tessa and
Teddy Eddy went into the house.

cakes

crisps

rolls

"I have some cakes,"
said Teddy Eddy,
"and some crisps, too!"

Tessa and Tim helped to
make some rolls.

Teddy Tim
looked up
at the clock.
"Time for
our picnic,
teddy bears!"
he said.

clock

"There is too much food to
carry in my basket!" said Tim.

All the teddy bears helped
to carry the food.

"Where are we going to eat the picnic?" Teddy Tessa asked.

field

"Come with me!" said Teddy Tim.

He took them to a big field. "We can sit here," he said.

grass

Teddy Tessa put a cloth on the grass.

Teddy Eddy put all the food on the cloth.

cloth

"That butterfly likes the cakes!" he said.

butterfly

"We **all** like the cakes,"
said Teddy Tessa.

eyes

bee

nose

ear

Everyone had fun at the picnic. They ate all the food.

"I feel sleepy," said Teddy Tim.

He shut his eyes.
A bee buzzed near his nose!
A butterfly sat on his ear!

Teddy Tessa and
Teddy Eddy put
everything away.

"Teddy Tim can carry it all
in his basket now," said Eddy.
"It is time to go home."

But he couldn't find a way to
wake up Teddy Tim.

Teddy Tessa and Teddy Eddy had to carry Teddy Tim all the way home!

Picture dictionary

Now you can read these words!

bananas

basket

bed

bee

butterfly

cakes

cherries

clock

cloth

crisps

cupboard

ears and eyes

 field

 fridge

 garden

 gate

 grass

 house

 juice

 melon

 nose

 plums

 road

 rolls

 shop

 sky

 sun